CW00853531

MEET ALL THESE FRIENDS IN BUZZ BOOKS:

Thomas the Tank Engine
The Animals of Farthing Wood
James Bond Junior
Fireman Sam
Joshua Jones
Bugs Bunny
Flintstones
Rupert
Babar

First published in Great Britain 1993
by Buzz Books, an imprint of Reed Children's Books
Michelin House, 81 Fulham Road, London SW3 6RB
and Auckland, Melbourne, Singapore and Toronto

Copyright © 1993 Eon Productions Limited, Mac B Inc.
Copyright © 1991 Danjaq, Inc. and United Artists Corporation
Text copyright © 1993 Reed International Books Limited
Illustrations copyright © 1993 Reed International Books Limited
Text adapted from an original cartoon entitled *Weather or Not*.
All rights reserved.

A CIP catalogue record for this book is available at the British Library.

ISBN 1 85591 288 0

Printed in Italy by Olivotto

Freeze Frame

Story adapted by Caryn Jenner

Illustrations by Arkadia

On a sunny summer day, Odd Job waited outside the Bank of London.

"When do we hit the armoured van?" asked his companion.

"As soon as the snowstorm begins," Odd Job told him.

Just then, thick white flakes began to fall from the sky.

"Now!" said Odd Job, taking off on his jet-powered skis.

He fired his laser gun at the guards, who slipped in the snow, dropping their sacks.

"Stop!" yelled one of the guards, firing back at Odd Job.

But Odd Job and the S.C.U.M. agent were already speeding across the snow with the sacks of money.

7

That evening at Warfield Academy,
James Bond Junior and his roommate
watched the news on television.

"A summer snowstorm?!" I.Q. exclaimed
as their friend, Wendy Day, gave the
Channel Six weather report.

"But only near the Bank of London,"
said James thoughtfully.

"Where robbers hijacked an armoured van and escaped on jet-powered skis," I.Q. added. "Sounds as if someone's been fiddling with the National Weather Satellite."

"Someone like S.C.U.M., you mean!" James exclaimed. "We'd better pack for a weekend in London, I.Q."

9

Odd Job and his boss, Goldfinger, counted the money from the bank robbery.

"Excellent," said Goldfinger, gazing at the cash on the table. "Odd Job, tomorrow we shall break into the Weather Centre again. Then we'll steal the most valuable prize of all — the Crown Jewels!"

That night in their London hotel, I.Q. showed James a few of his latest inventions.

"I.Q., I'm not sure what I'll use these things for," said James as he examined the gadgets. "But at least I'll be prepared!"

11

Later that night, Wendy rang James with an urgent message.

There's been a break-in at the Weather Centre!

As James and Wendy approached the Weather Centre in the Channel Six helicopter, they suddenly entered another summer snowstorm.

"Look!" said Wendy, pointing to a dark figure on a snowmobile.

Flinching against the fierce blizzard, James climbed out of the helicopter and down the rope ladder, stretching his legs towards the speeding machine.

But Odd Job was ready. Quickly, he leaped off the snowmobile and onto a ledge. Then he tossed his steel-rimmed hat at the rope ladder, slicing right through it!

James felt himself falling....

James landed in the soft snow. "That's cold!" he exclaimed, scrambling to his feet.

The pilot landed the helicopter in a snow-covered car park.

"Odd Job got away," James told Wendy.

Wendy grinned. "No, he didn't. I saw him go into the Weather Centre."

James and Wendy tried the door to the
Weather Centre. It was unlocked.

"Where's the guard?" asked Wendy.

Just then, Goldfinger and Odd Job stepped
out of the shadows.

"We're guarding the Weather Centre
tonight — from young meddlers like you
two!" said Goldfinger, aiming his laser gun
at James.

He led James and Wendy to a room marked *Arctic Chamber*.

"Enjoy your stay in the deep freeze!" said Goldfinger, sniggering wickedly.

"J-James, what are we g-going to do?" asked Wendy, between chattering teeth.

James was already busy. With numb fingers, he pulled out I.Q.'s repelling magnet and pointed it at the door lock. The metal pin on the other side of the door clattered to the floor.

"Goldfinger isn't such a cool customer after all!" said James as he and Wendy stepped into the warmth of the corridor.

W-What are you doing?

With I.Q.'s repelling magnet, we should be able to unlock the door.

On Channel Six the next morning, Wendy reported snow, sleet, rain, wind, thunder and lightning.

James and I.Q. were at the TV station, where I.Q. was working on the computer.

"If I can break the code, I'll be able to reprogram the weather satellite," said I.Q.

"Good luck, old chum," James replied.
"In the meantime, Wendy and I will take
the helicopter to the Tower of London.
Goldfinger has always wanted a chance at
the Crown Jewels, and this weather is the
perfect cover to steal them — unless
Wendy and I can stop him!"

Through the heavy sleet and snow, James and Wendy saw a satellite dish perched on one of the turrets of the Tower of London.

"Look! That must be where Goldfinger controls the weather satellite," said James.

As Wendy prepared to land the helicopter on the roof of the Tower, a sudden gust of wind caught the propeller, causing the helicopter to whirl about out of control!

Finally, the 'copter dipped toward the ground and Wendy cut the engines.

"Jump!" she shouted to James.

Once again, James landed in the soft snow. He looked up to see the helicopter burst into a ball of flame.

James and Wendy decided to climb up the Tower and surprise Goldfinger, but I.Q.'s super-stick pads were no match for the crazy weather that the evil villain had whipped up with the weather satellite.

"James, I'm losing my grip!" said Wendy.

"We'll have to go inside," James replied.

He used his magnetic repelling pen to turn the infra-red security alarm away from the window, then he cut through the plate glass with the mini-saw built into the pen.

"I guess this weather has discouraged the tourists," James whispered as they climbed through the window into the dark, deserted armoury.

Quickly and quietly, James and Wendy
made their way through the maze of
exhibits in the armoury. As they neared the
steps leading to the turret, they heard the
clink of metal.

"Look out, James!" shouted Wendy as a
knight in shining armour jumped out from
one of the exhibits and attacked, taking
James by surprise.

24

"You're no match for me, Bond," said
Odd Job, taking off his helmet. He looked
round for his steel-rimmed bowler hat, but
Wendy was quicker.

"I'm a champion with a frisbee, Odd Job.
Put James down, or I'll toss your deadly
hat — at you!"

"I wouldn't do that if I were you,"
threatened a voice from behind.

At Channel Six, I.Q. was still working at the computer.

"Of course!" he exclaimed, pushing several buttons. "I'll program the computer to retract the solar panels, then the weather satellite won't have any power left."

I've broken the code. Now I just have to reprogram the computer.

Far above Earth, the satellite continued its orbit, but without the solar panels, it lost the power to control the weather.

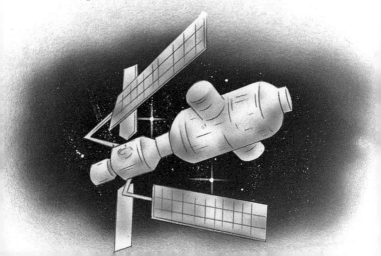

At the Tower of London, a ray of sunshine suddenly streamed into the armoury.

"What's happening? It's not supposed to be sunny in London!" Goldfinger snapped as he glanced at the window.

James and Wendy saw their chance. Wendy tossed Odd Job's hat at Goldfinger. Goldfinger ducked, but in the scuffle with James, he dropped the laser gun.

"I'd say your golden days are over, Goldfinger," said James, picking up the laser gun.

He pressed the security alarm, and within seconds, the police arrived. They arrested Goldfinger and Odd Job, as well as a pair of S.C.U.M. agents who were caught attempting to steal the Crown Jewels.

James and Wendy walked outside.

"You know, I've never been so glad to see the sun," said Wendy, breathing in the warm summer air.

"I agree," said James with a grin. "Perhaps I.Q. could program the weather satellite so that the sun shines over London a bit more often!"

29